Stranded in a Snowstorm

STRANDED IN A SNOWSTORM

Published in New York, New York, by Morgan James Publishing. Morgan James and The Entrepreneurial Publisher are trademarks of Morgan James, LLC. www.MorganJamesPublishing.com

The Morgan James Speakers Group can bring authors to your live event. For more information or to book an event visit The Morgan James Speakers Group at www.TheMorganJamesSpeakersGroup.com.

A **free** eBook edition is available with the purchase of this print book.

CLEARLY PRINT YOUR NAME ABOVE IN UPPER CASE

Instructions to claim your free eBook edition:
1. Download the BitLit app for Android or iOS
2. Write your name in **UPPER CASE** on the line
3. Use the BitLit app to submit a photo
4. Download your eBook to any device

ISBN 9781630471736 paperback
ISBN 9781630471743 eBook
ISBN 9781630471750 hardcover
Library of Congress Control Number:

Cover Illustration by:
Mike Webber

Interior Design by:
Chris Treccani
www.3dogdesign.net

Author Photo by:
Kevin Ryan

In an effort to support local communities, raise awareness and funds, Morgan James Publishing donates a percentage of all book sales for the life of each book to Habitat for Humanity Peninsula and Greater Williamsburg.

Get involved today, visit
www.MorganJamesBuilds.com

Habitat
for Humanity
Peninsula and
Greater Williamsburg
Building Partner

Ride on!

STRANDED IN A SNOWSTORM!

Paul R Woz

A NOVEL BY **PAUL WOZNIAK**

NEW YORK

Ride on!

This story contains situations that occur in the wilderness and the backcountry, and should not be attempted by those who do not have experience and expertise in Nature, especially in avalanche country. Respect the wilderness. Respect your life. The goal is always to live to play another day. The woods and mountains can be a dangerous place for those who are not skilled in dealing with Nature.

It can even be dangerous for those who are.

Pack it in. Pack it out. Leave only footsteps behind.

This book is for you.

CHAPTER 1

Nico's mother was listening to the news a few hours after she sent her son on a backpacking trip with his babysitter, Hannah.

"This just in," said the reporter. *"A blizzard of epic proportions is set to smother the entire region. The area will be covered in snow by tomorrow morning. Police are asking that people not travel unless it is absolutely necessary."*

Snow in May? Nico's mom ran for her phone. She frantically dialed Hannah. Voice mail. Hannah and Nico had boasted of a "technology free trip" so she wouldn't be able to reach them. They were headed right into the middle of a storm, and there was no way to warn them.

* * * * *

Meanwhile, Nico and Hannah had just parked the car high in the Rocky Mountains at the trailhead. They were getting ready to go and were doing a very thorough equipment check. On this backpacking trip, they would carry everything they needed with them. If they left anything behind, they'd have to do without it.

Food, clothing and shelter are the things all humans need to survive . . . but tech stuff is not, so they had decided to leave all their tech toys at home. Hannah never went anywhere or did anything without her smartphone, and Nico was the same way with his. They both thought it would be special to leave them behind and go *old school* for a few days. Hannah and Nico both loved their devices. But phones are not necessary for survival, and they both thought it would be pretty cool to go "off the grid" for once— they wanted the bare-bones experience. So, they were leaving their devices behind for this special backcountry trip.

"Nico, you don't have a phone . . . and I turned mine off before we left," she said as she chucked her phone in the glove box of the car. "So it's just us, our gear and our Mother Nature until we get back. Will you put on your shoes, please?"

"I didn't bring any," said Nico.

"All you have are your sandals?" Hannah asked.

"I love my sandals."

"I do, too, Nico, but it's going to be cold tonight. You don't have any shoes at all?"

"Nope." Nico smiled mischievously. He was a confident kid that lived a kind of idyllic existence in a cool town in Colorado. Sometimes, he was too confident.

"Dude. Not good." Hannah paused, wondering if this was a big enough deal to cause them to have to go back. "Well, I have extra socks you can wear. I'll give them to you at the campsite. Let's go!"

"Whoopty doopty doo!" replied Nico.

* * * * *

Nico and Hannah headed up the trail. It was warm in the morning sunlight. Strolling through the woods, they had a special feeling that cannot be found in a town. Even though we rely on our "creature comforts," we all have a connection to nature, a place without the internet, electricity, plumbing, or even houses. Our bodies feel wonderful when we are totally surrounded by nature because it is a special place where everything is right where it should be.

Each step took them closer and closer to the goal of their hike—the top of a mountain at over 13,000 feet in the Colorado Rockies. They wanted to reach the summit simply because it feels amazing to stand on the very top of a large mountain. But it was a long way up. The walk would take more than four hours.

About two hours in, Hannah noticed something strange.

"Looks like a snow sky." A snow sky is a deep gray sky that seems to hang very low to the ground; it has a cramped, tight feeling to it. This was a strange sight for them to see since it was almost summer. However, in Colorado a May snowstorm is always possible, especially at high elevations.

"Is it supposed to snow?" asked Nico.

"No. Sunny and low 60s was the forecast, right?" They had both checked the weather before the trip, a must before any outdoor "*radventure.*"

"That's what I saw," said Nico. "There was a storm over the ski resorts in Utah. I know because they are still reporting powder days, but it wasn't supposed to make it this far over." Nico loved to ride his snowboard, so he checked the powder reports from the fall through the spring. He had also learned in his school how important it is to plan for safety on trips into the woods like this. "Low 60's, maybe upper 50's during the day, 30's at night with no rain or snow in the forecast."

There is an old saying, "If you don't like the weather in Colorado, just wait an hour." Hannah fought the urge to believe what she was seeing and decided to continue on. Another must in the wilderness is that we trust our best instinct. This time, Hannah did not.

CHAPTER 2

Back at Nico's house, his mother was on the phone trying to find someone to help. The police and fire department wouldn't help her because, technically, Nico and Hannah weren't lost. Plus, they were short on officers and firefighters because they were preparing for the snowstorm. Just when she was almost in a state of total panic, she looked up from the phone in her hand to a picture on the wall, and there she saw the one person she knew that could help—their good friend Paul. The picture that caught her gaze was of her, Nico, Hannah, and Paul. They were all smiling from the fun they had just had on a whitewater rafting trip. The four of them were all decked out in their river gear, paddles in hand, with each of their arms around the others shoulders.

Nico was her only son, and Hannah was their neighbor. She was a college student, but had been watching Nico since she was twelve and he was four. Paul came into the scene a few years ago when Nico started at his outdoor expeditionary style elementary school. He was a volunteer guide for many of the trips that the kids took, and they just loved him. Nico thought he was the coolest because he sang and played guitar in a band called *The Green Minstrels* and was a skater, skier, snowboarder, kayaker, climber and all around extreme sports nut. Plus, Paul just had a way of making people know that he understood them. It was hard to describe, but it's kind of like when you meet someone and you know you will become friends, or that you would do favors for each other. Paul was like that with almost everyone, and he treated kids just like he treated adults.

Whether or not Nico liked him didn't matter right now. What did count was that, with Paul's experience in the mountains and wilderness, he would be able to help. Hearing the situation, he didn't even hesitate before he said, "I'm on my way."

* * * * *

Before any trip into the woods, smart trekkers always show someone else *exactly* where they are going on a map. Nico and Hannah did this, so his mom was able to show Paul where he needed to look for them. The snow had already started to fall.

"It's a four-hour drive and it's going to snow the whole time. It's another four-hour trek in, so by then I'll have to have my skis on. That's steep terrain, so Nordic skis won't work."

Nordic skiing is also known as cross country, and is good for traveling across flat or slightly hilly terrain. The Rocky Mountains are anything but flat.

"I'm gonna have to bring my skins and my alpine touring rig," Paul said. Alpine touring rigs are special setups that allow skiers and snowboarders to climb mountains without the need of a chairlift. The skins are special, sticky liners that attach to the bottom of skis that let the ski grab the snow to go up a hill. Once at the top, they peel the skin off the ski, and then it's all fresh powder on the way down. "I'll drag a sled that has Hannah and Nico's splitboards and boots." Splitboards are snowboards that are modified to split apart down the middle and turn into skis. Then they can be used to walk up snowy hills in the backcountry. "Plus I'll bring food, warm gear and all kinds of other goodies."

Nico's mom looked absolutely terrified. He smiled.

"Don't you worry. Those two will be fine! They have shelter and sleeping bags, and Hannah knows what she is doing out there. There is no reason why they should be in any immediate danger, no matter how much snow we see tonight. They've got food, they'll know to make fire and hunker down. Hannah will make sure they stay put and I'll go in there and get them out. It may even be fun! We're going to make some turns in May!"

Skiers and snowboarders often refer to their sports as *making turns,* since that is essentially what they do, over and over again.

Nico's mom was still scared. "Can Nico receive texts on his phone?" Paul asked.

"Yes, but they said they weren't taking their devices with them," Nico's mother replied.

"I know what they said, but if I were twelve years old, my phone or device might *accidentally* find its way into my pack." They both smiled, happy for the ornery predictability of kids.

"Send Nico a text and tell them to turn around right away. Maybe he'll get it. Also let them know I'm on my way, in case they don't get it in time."

The text from Nico's mom didn't cause a buzz because the device was powered down. But, just like they thought, Nico had stashed it in his pack just in case Hannah thought it would be a good idea to play a few games later.

CHAPTER 3

The sky grew grayer over the trail, and the snow started falling shortly after. At this point they had hiked three hours from the road and were nearing the summit. Mountaintops are beautiful but dangerous places. Trees can't grow above 11,500 feet, and the plants and grass that do exist are very hardy and tough. The wind blows, and the air is thin, so it's hard to breathe, much less hike. Weather is very extreme high in the Rocky Mountains.

Hannah looked up at a smothering, gray cloud. She could barely see the outline of the mountain peak. Little snowflakes floated in the air and the wind was starting to pick up. She decided they needed to stop. "I don't want to go up there. It looks gnarly."

"That's a bummer. But I think you're right," Nico said. Just then, the wind roared! They started moving quickly to get back down to the trees.

"This doesn't feel like a little snowstorm!" Nico had to yell at Hannah over the wind. The snow swirled sideways through the air. Dust and little rocks blew and felt like a thousand tiny razors cutting into their faces. Squinting, they had to hurry far into the trees before they felt any relief.

All of a sudden, it began to *dump*. It was like the sky opened up and was dropping onto them. At first they had the natural reaction to giggle at the late spring snow. But as Hannah walked along, she started to become concerned.

"Nico, I think we should head back to the car," she said.

"Are you kidding me? The car is four hours away! We'll never make it in the daylight."

"I know. I think we should keep walking *through the dark*." she looked at him to let him know she was serious.

"Through the dark? Why? That's crazy!"

"I know, but I think this weather may be crazier. Nothing that I saw predicted snow, and it's dumping. I think the weather has changed and we could be seeing a major storm. If we are, then we have no idea how much will fall, but we both know it could be a lot. If we're lucky, maybe we just get a dusting. But we could end up with a couple feet on the ground. Look," she said, motioning to the ground. "The trail is already starting to blend in with the rest of the woods. It won't be long before it disappears. And you are wearing sandals."

Nico froze, and looked down at his feet. *Oops.* He wanted to punch himself in the face for his stupidity. He was totally into prep and safety and making sure that he was ready for every circumstance when he went out into the wilderness. He was so into it, some of the kids teased him about it. They called him 'Captain Backcountry'. All he ever wanted for his birthday and Christmas was camping, hiking, snowboarding and climbing gear, and here he was, miles away from the road without the proper *shoes.* Man, he felt bad.

"Nico," Hannah said, and actually smiled, "shame isn't going to help us. No blame, no shame, no justification allowed. What has happened has happened, now it's time to deal with it without feeling bad. Feeling bad about it accomplishes nothing." He looked at Hannah and attempted a smile. She always harped on 'personal responsibility', saying things like "Everything that happens to us is our own fault, but if we mess up, there's no reason to get down on ourselves. No learning can happen when we are feeling shame." He loved that about her. Other teachers and grown ups always made kids feel bad when they did something wrong. Hannah was different. "We are going to be fine," she said. "We may get a little tired and we may get a little cold, but we are going to be fine." He nodded and took a deep breath.

"We have to think clearly and make *good* decisions," Hannah said gently. "Here's how I see it. If we walk out tonight it will suck and your feet will be cold and wet. If we hunker down and see what happens we could be stranded out here for a while. If that's the case, your mobility and much of what you can do will be limited because you only have sandals."

Nico nodded. It was hard for him not to feel bad since his stupid shoe choice could be the thing that really put them in danger.

"It's okay, Nico, kids *and* adults make these kinds of mistakes. It's almost summer and it was hot, so you wore your sandals. No biggie, but what we do now really counts. We should walk out. Who knows how much snow could fall while we sleep, but if it's more than an inch, it's going to cause you some real issues. If we keep walking we can probably beat most of it and be back in a warm car. Are you in?"

Tired from a long day's hike, Nico was not looking forward to hiking through the dark woods with headlamps.

However, he knew Hannah was making sense.

"I'm in," he said.

* * * * *

Paul was trying his best to drive up the mountain, but spring storms in Colorado can be crippling. The snow fell hard on the town all afternoon, and he spent most of the day in slushy, snarly traffic.

He couldn't just head out right away. Nico's mom helped him gather all the gear her son would need. Then he had to head to Hannah's to pick up her snowboard, snowboard boots, beacon, shovel, probe, jacket, pants and gloves. Paul didn't own a sled that he could use to tow their gear, so he had to borrow one, and he had to do all this while street crews were trying to clear the roads. Little accidents and fender benders were everywhere because of the conditions, and he was struggling to keep the list of all the things he needed in his head. By the time he gathered all the gear, the traffic was almost stopped. He had hoped to make it in before night, but now he knew he wouldn't be able to hit the trail until morning. It was slow going and he had a long trip ahead.

CHAPTER 4

Nico and Hannah had problems hiking out right away. The heavy snow turned the trail into a slick of mud. Every uphill climb was a battle. Every downhill descent was a slippery, sloppy slide. They weren't getting very far. They both fell numerous times, bumping knees and shins, scraping palms and feeling like they were in a craggy pit of grease.

Though he was only twelve years old, Nico had survival smarts. Sensing a scary situation, he spoke up.

"Hannah, we should set up camp somewhere that we can be seen." Nico had been taught that if he was ever lost in the woods, he should stay put in a place that could be seen from above or afar. Stay put, and work on being found. Make a big X on the ground with sticks and rocks that could be seen from an airplane or helicopter. Or write a big word like "HELP" or "SOS." Any pilot that sees that is sure to call it in or investigate because things like that are extremely noticeable to humans. Nature doesn't create many straight lines, so just making an "X" really stands out in the midst of a natural landscape.

Nico was also taught that having something to do in a

survival situation occupies the mind and steers it away from fear. Nico thought they should make many X's, or work on making one big one. The main thing was to keep busy and stay put, especially because they showed Nico's mom a map of exactly where they would be.

Hannah agreed. "You're right, Nico," she said. "It's so slippery and muddy that we'll never make it out tonight. This is *brutal*."

At that moment, they looked at each other and truly realized that they were all alone in the wilderness with no way out. Hannah let a small tear drop down her cheek. This alarmed Nico but he still trusted that Hannah would protect him. And he would protect her, too. It was scary, but at least they were together. Hannah snapped out of it quickly.

"Well, we were going to sleep in the woods anyway, so it's not like our plan has changed," Hannah said, working her way back to her usual cheerful self. "We're just going to sleep in the woods in the snow! It looks like there is a meadow up ahead. Let's check that out." They walked along.

"Yeah," said Nico, "this isn't really any different than what we'd planned before." A protective instinct awoke in

Nico that he hadn't felt before. Since he was a small child with Hannah, she had always been in charge. As he grew older, they became kind of a team. They just went and had fun together, even though, officially, she was still 'babysitting' him. Now that they were in a survival situation, he knew that he was as responsible for them as she was. He brought skills that she didn't have, and he knew he needed to be able to take care of things that she couldn't. "We're still on the trail, so if it doesn't snow too much we can probably follow the trail's impression tomorrow morning."

"Maybe. It would be better to avoid any *famous last words* type scenarios, though," said Hannah.

"What do you mean?"

"Famous last words. Like, 'We'll be fine!' or 'Let's just do it.' That's a way a lot of people don't make it back. They think they can go off the trail for just a little bit. They hear a waterfall just off in the distance, and just want to leave the trail to go find it. Or, unlike us, they decide to keep walking even though the snow has already hidden the trail." They looked around and realized that it was snowing hard enough that they could no longer tell what was trail and what wasn't.

"See?" Hannah said. "Playing in the woods in the West is no joke. The wilderness is so big! You could walk for days without coming across a road, much less a person. The problem is that everything looks the same. It's all trees, dirt rocks, plants and grasses. It stretches forever, and that is both the amazing and dangerous thing about it. When we play in it, we take a chance, but that's what our gear is for. What clothes did you pack?"

One of Nico's favorite parts about backpacking was packing his pack. He loved that if he brought just the right amount of the right items, he could go as far as he wanted into the woods and still be just fine. "Well, besides a questionable choice of footgear, I am pretty stoked on my stuff. I have a bunch of socks, a long-sleeve t-shirt, a fleece and my jacket, plus a beanie. I brought a flint with a striker attached to it, my multi-tool, a compass, an emergency blanket, a few different lights with plenty of batteries…lots of stuff." He smiled and he thought of his smartphone buried deep in his pack. He felt a pang of guilt for going back on his word and decided not to mention it.

The meadow opened up to them. Though their tent would take the full brunt of the snowstorm, they had a big, flat spot to set up camp.

"Nice. You won't need that stuff for a little while. You'll be plenty warm, because guess what time it is?"

"What time?"

"It's FIREWOOD time!" Hannah smiled.

* * * * *

As Nico brought back armload after armload of firewood, he remembered what Paul told him. "*Gather up about as much as you think you'll need . . . then go collect 20 times that much. You'll need a pile as big as two of your tents to make it through a cold night. There is nothing worse than fumbling around in the dark looking for firewood.*" So Nico just kept tromping around, collecting firewood. His toes were very cold and hurting from the brush, because his sandals offered no protection or warmth to his toes. The socks he was wearing didn't help.

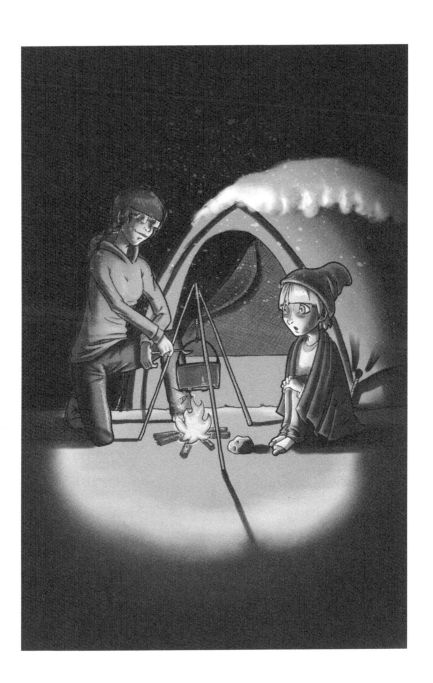

The snow fell, almost two inches an hour. Nico gathered wood while Hannah made their fire and boiled snow to make water. He kept gathering until Hannah told him their meal was ready to eat.

They ate dehydrated food made just for the backcountry. It was very easy to make: They simply had to add boiling water, mix and let it set for a few minutes. Since they had no idea how long they'd be out, they split one packet of beef and noodles, and saved the others. After such a long, cold day of hiking it was delicious and really hit the spot. Still, they'd used a lot of energy and it left them a little hungry.

Hiking through mountainous woods burns hundreds, even thousands, of calories. Add heavy packs to the situation, and they burned even more energy. Since they had to carry everything they would need, their packs weighed almost 40 pounds. For the body to function properly, those burned calories needed to be replaced. The amount they had eaten didn't replace all the calories they had lost but they had no idea how long they would be stranded out there. So they had to ration their food, just in case. Even the idea of not being able to eat all they wanted let them know that they were in a serious situation. Hannah kept boiling snow for water.

Then they went out into the meadow and made an X with sticks and rocks, but quickly realized that it was pointless. The snow had the first part of the X covered before they finished the second part. If they were going to be seen from above, it wouldn't be like this.

Just before bed she took an old sweatshirt and flattened it out near the fire. She rolled a stone from the fire ring onto the shirt and picked it up by collecting the outsides of the shirt, forming a sort of bag. "Don't touch the rock," she said, handing it to Nico. "It's super hot." She took another shirt and did it again. They took the rocks into the tent to warm it up a little bit, being careful not to let them make contact with the bottom of the tent. If the steaming hot rock did touch the tent, it would sear right through it, so they kept them in the cotton shirts. After the rocks cooled a bit, they kept them wrapped in the shirts and put them in their sleeping bags.

Surprisingly, it wasn't a bad night. They knew that nights were always cold high in the Rocky Mountains, so they had brought burly sleeping bags and warm layers of clothes. Their tent was all-season, so it was sealed against the wind. Just their body heat raised the temperature inside.

Plus, they heard silence like they'd never known. The

storm brought a blanket of white and peace. Fresh snow is one of the most special things on this beautiful Earth. They slept well after a long, cold, frightening day.

CHAPTER 5

Paul made it to the trailhead around midnight. *"Six inches of snow has fallen and this is expected to continue through tonight and well into tomorrow..."* said the man on the radio as he arrived.

He parked right next to Hannah's car. *Six inches my foot!* he thought. *It looks more like twelve.* Well, that guy was probably giving the snow totals for the town, which was about 5,000 feet in elevation below the trailhead. Areas that are higher in the mountains always receive more snow, colder temps, and tougher weather overall, so Paul wasn't surprised that, at high altitude, the snow was really piling up.

Weather in the Rockies was curious. Mountaintops just half an hour apart could receive completely different amounts of snow. Skiers and snowboarders knew this all too well. While people at Steamboat Resort might be waist or even face deep in fresh powder, folks in Summit County, just 2 hours and one mountain pass away, might only be riding in dust on crust.

Either way, there was a lot of snow. As much as Paul wanted to go into the woods that night, he knew better. It doesn't do any good if the rescuer needs to be rescued. Dark, snowy woods are too dangerous for travel. He'd have to wait until morning. He put the back seats down in his mini SUV and climbed into the back for a rest. The morning would bring a lot of work.

As he prepared to sleep in his car, he thought of all the times he had come to this very spot for fun. He had never been there with any of his friends in danger. He hiked there, skied there, camped and climbed rocks, but had never been there with only rescue in mind. It made the parking lot sign look different. The information that usually was just a part of the landscape now represented the only piece of civilization besides the road in the whole area. Everything else was uncivilized. Unpaved. Dangerous. Settling in to his mummy bag, he made an attempt to think happy thoughts. He envisioned himself finding his friends with no problems, and the smiles they would share when he did.

CHAPTER 6

Nico and Hannah awoke to total silence. They were cold but they weren't freezing, and they had slept well. When they arose and looked out, they could see how high the snow was piled on their tent. They could barely believe it. Hannah had to *poof* out the sides a couple times before she was able to zip it down all the way without piles of snow falling right into the tent. There were almost two feet of snow on the ground.

Their campfire from the night before had gone totally out. They went to work on it right away. Fire has the amazing effect of making any survival situation much better. It provides life and limb-saving heat. It boils water to purify it in the wild.

Almost every source of water in the wild should be considered dangerous. Rivers and lakes usually have bacteria in them that can make us very sick. Even if the water comes right from snowy peaks as it does in the Rockies, or directly from a glacier, wild animals can poop in it or die in it and cause horrible illnesses that can put a person down for days or weeks. Giardia is one of the most common illnesses, and the most miserable. It makes a person vomit and have diarrhea that can actually cause severe weight loss.

That is why fire is one of the most important forces of nature that humans have ever harnessed. Right now, it was doing many important things at once for Nico and Hannah. It changed snow into water. It provided warmth, without which they might have frozen the night before. It provided food and drink, like the hot tea they made to help warm up their insides and make them feel more human in the harsh, cold wilderness. It also kept predators like mountain lions away from their camp. All things considered, they were in a very good situation, even though it was still dangerous and frightening.

For breakfast they split a dehydrated Western omelet, and it was delicious. After they had the fire going, Nico looked up at the sky and realized that it was still snowing. There wasn't a trace of sun or blue. It was still cramped and gray.

* * * * *

Paul was preparing to ski in to find his friends. He had a pair of climbing skins that stuck to the bottom of his downhill skis. Skins allow skiers and splitboarders to climb snowy mountains. Cut to the exact shape of the ski, one side is sticky and simply sticks on the bottom of the ski. They're kind of like the skin of a fish: Rub a hand across one way, from the toe or front of the ski to the back, and it is smooth. Rub the other way and it is rough. This allows the toe of one ski to slide ahead, and the other to grab so that the adventurers can push themselves forward. Without skins, climbing a snowy mountain on downhill skis is about as effective as trying to swim up a waterfall.

Special alpine touring bindings allowed his heel to lift so he could walk up hill through the snow. Normal alpine bindings keep the toe and the heel firmly attached to the ski. Since his heel was free, it was almost like walking. When he came to a big downhill, he could click his bindings back to normal, remove the skins and ski just like he would at a resort. He had secured a sled to his waist, and it carried all the survival supplies three people would possibly need.

Even though it was very cold out, Paul wore only a thin t-shirt and fleece; once he started moving, the activity would heat up his body very quickly. Sweating in the cold can be very dangerous: If his body was covered with moisture and he stopped moving and generating that body heat, the moisture would freeze instantly and could cause hypothermia. To prevent that, he wore special wool clothing that released moisture and heat. Wool is a great outdoor fiber because it dries quickly and allows the skin to breathe. Even when it is wet, it holds in heat. Paul spent much of his life in the snowy woods, so he was ready for this.

However, the fresh snow erased any signs of the trail. Everything looked the same—just spruce, pine and aspen trees jutting out of the snow. Luckily, before he left he and Nico's mom synced his phone to be able to use the GPS tracking app to locate Nico's phone. This showed the device's exact geographical location. When he arrived at the trailhead, he could see that it wasn't in their car: It was blinking about four miles away in the middle of the national forest.

Paul laughed. "I knew he'd take it with him!" Though Nico and Hannah went backpacking to be in nature without any devices, technology would be what would save them.

* * * * *

Nico and Hannah took stock of their situation. Nico wanted to get moving right away, but Hannah wasn't so sure.

"If we hike out your feet will be in two feet of snow for over five hours. We don't have enough clothing to make you better footwear, and I'm afraid you could end up with frostbite. If you had shoes, it could be fine, but all you have are sandals." Frostbite happens when parts of the body, like fingers or toes, begin to freeze. In really bad cases, the blood freezes and the fingers and toes have to be removed. It only happens in the worst of conditions, but in Nico and Hannah's case, it was possible.

"We have to wait for someone to come and get us, or until it warms up," said Hannah.

"So what do we do?" Nico asked

"We build a big fire and have some fun here! We have enough food to spread out for more than four days. We have warmth and shelter, and we'll keep drying socks for you to change into. We have plenty of snow to melt so we won't run out of water. Nico, we may walk out of here, but it's not going to be today. It's too cold."

"But what if it snows so much that we can't ever get out of here?" Nico was becoming very frightened.

"That will not happen. Nico, we will be fine, I promise! The most important thing in survival is your *attitude!* This can't beat us. In fact, you are going to have a great story for when you go back to school."

Thinking of his friends at school made Nico feel so much better, he almost laughed. He was moving from elementary to middle school next year, so he thought that surviving this crazy experience could give him some much needed cred in the hallways. He went to a special school that took kids on long trips each year. Many of them were backcountry trips, so his friends would understand what it would be like to be stranded on the side of a snowy mountain for a few days. To be sure, though, the story that Nico would take back with him to school would seem much more frightening than what he was really facing!

Hannah's pep talk worked: Nico was starting to believe that they were going to be fine. Feeling better, Nico spoke in a teasing tone. "So I guess you won't be mad that I brought my phone now, so we can kill some time? Maybe shoot a few selfies to remember the moment?"

Hannah's head snapped around and she looked at Nico. "You brought it?"

"Yeah," Nico said defensively. He thought she was mad. "Sorry!"

"Nico, that's wonderful!!" Hannah sang and grabbed him and gave him a big hug. "It has GPS in it, right? Maybe we'll be able to send a text! Oh, Nico, I have never been so happy that you went back on your word!"

"I just wanted to play Fruit Ninja," said Nico. "You can play Fruit Ninja and still enjoy the woods."

"You are so right, Nico! Oh, I'm so glad." Hannah squeezed him tight. "And from now on, you can bring it everywhere we go."

Nico dug into his pack and produced his smartphone. His mom and dad let him have it as long as he mowed the grass every week, raked leaves in the fall, and shoveled snow in the winter. If he did it on time, they paid for texting and data. If not, they didn't pay.

He powered it up. "Fresh battery. I knew it wouldn't see a plug for a few days." Right after it booted it gave a *buzz-bing*. Two text messages. The first one he knew was his mom because he had customized her text tone. At first he had made it quack like a duck, but his mom heard it and wasn't flattered, so he changed it to the delicate *ding* sound that she liked better. The other was his general tone that could have been anyone.

The first one from his mom read, "*HUGE SNOWSTORM ON THE WAY. TURN AROUND NOW!!!*"

Nico and Hannah looked at each other. "They tried to

warn us," said Hannah.

The next message was from Paul.

"A video message!" cried Nico.

The smiling face of their hat-wearing friend Paul appeared on the screen. *"Howdy friends! Whoopty doopty doo! I guess you didn't expect this snow. I didn't either! Don't you worry, I'm on my way in to get you. Just stay put, stay warm, make LOTS of water, and I'll be there as soon as I can."*

"Paul is on the way," said Hannah. "We are saved!"

"Whoopty doopty doo!" Nico hollered, and he never meant those words more.

* * * * *

Even following a clear tracking signal, Paul was having a hard time. Snow hid the trail, so he started traveling *as the crow flies*. "As the crow flies" is an old saying that means a straight line from one point to another. Crows and other birds can fly this way, yes, but animals and humans usually take the *easiest* path. That's why roads, especially in hilly and mountainous areas, are curvy. They have to wrap around natural obstacles like peaks, water, valleys and private land.

The trail Nico and Hannah had traveled was a tough hike into the mountains, but it was still walkable. However Paul made the mistake of trying to go directly from his location to Nico and Hannah's location in a straight line according to the visual on the map: He soon found himself navigating deep ravines, climbing steep hills, and running into impassably tight groves of trees. He was adding hours to an already difficult trip, skinning through deep, fresh snow while dragging a sled with 70 pounds of supplies.

This is just another example of how important making good, *slow* decisions can be in an emergency situation. The best survival tool we have is our brain, and it does not work in a state of fear or panic. Paul was drenched in sweat, and it was hard to constantly take out his phone to make sure he was on the right track. It was slow going, and it was getting late.

* * * * *

After a full day and a half of clouds and snow, the sun had finally appeared. It created a western skyline that was beautiful for Hannah and Nico to see, but now it was late afternoon and Paul still hadn't arrived. The stranded backpackers grew uneasy. Soon it would be dark.

Hannah and Nico decided to blow on the emergency whistles they had strapped on their packs with carabiners. If Paul was having trouble finding them, the whistle would let him hear them from much further than screaming would, and would save their voices, too.

They spread out to the outskirts of their camp to blow their whistles.

"TWEEEEEEEEEEEEEEEEEEEEEEEET!"   Nico blew expectantly.

"TWEET! TWEET! TWEEEEEEEEEEEET!" Hannah blew rhythmically. It helped to keep her spirits up.

"TWEEEEEEEEEEEEEEEEEEEEEEEEEEET!"   Nico blew long and loud, hoping that longer was better.

Suddenly, Nico thought he heard a muffled whistle somewhere in the wind. He stopped blowing and cupped both his hands to his ears. There it was again! Nico blasted a long powerful whistle.

Hannah heard the difference in the volume of Nico's whistle and looked over.

"I think I heard him!" Nico hollered. She could barely hear him because they were far away from each other. But his body language was obvious, so she started making her way over to him.

"I can hear someone Hannah!" Nico said as she joined him.

"TWEEEEEEEEEEEEEEEEEEEEEEEEEEEEEEEEE EEEEEEEET!"

The sound was coming from above them on the ridge. They could both hear the sound of Paul's whistle now, and they returned it with loud steady honks on their own mini-horns.

Hannah and Nico stood arm in arm, their eyes welling up as they listened to Paul playfully whistling, "Tweet, tweet,

tweet. Tweety, tweety, tweet." Only Paul would turn a survival search and rescue situation into a song. His hat appeared over the ridge, and his body and sled followed.

"Hello!" they heard him bellow. He was too far away to talk to them. He started toward them and then noticed it was all downhill. He held up one finger as if to say, "One moment," and started taking off some of his gear.

"He's taking off his skins so he can ski to us!"

Nico and Hannah looked at each other and burst into tears and laughter. They hugged, and Nico looked at his feet. They had been freezing since the first night.

They looked up as Paul was clicking his boots into his skis. Once he was done, he dipped into his first powder turn and skied with control of the big heavy sled down to his friends.

"Hello, my friends! What are you doing out here in the snow?" the trio hugged. They laughed and caught each other up to speed on what they had seen and experienced and actually felt good about the situation. No, that's not right. They felt *great*.

CHAPTER 7

It was too late to hike out so, after sending a text to let Nico's mom know that they were together, and barring any crazy turns of events, they'd be out of the woods by tomorrow, they took advantage of the remaining natural daylight to gather plenty of firewood and make the campsite more comfortable for the night. Paul had brought tarps, extra sleeping bags, snowshoes and a camp hatchet. He also had brought the most important thing to Nico, his snowboard boots.

"I was helpless in these sandals," Nico said as he slid them on. "Ahhh! That feels so good! I will never try to hike in sandals again!"

Hannah shuffled through the gear in the sled. "Dude, you brought my splitboard? Bueno! And my skins! You are the man!" She put on her boots, turned her snowboard into skis and attached her skins to the bottom. Then she took a hatchet and went into the woods. She cut some low hanging spruce branches and had Nico take them back to the campsite. After that, she found a rotting log that was turning to a gritty mush called pumice and chopped it up. She heaped mounds of the pumice onto the tarp and dragged it carefully back to the campsite. They took down the tent and put the spruce boughs down on the wet ground. Then they put the soft pumice on top of that to fill in the gaps between the branches. Together, the boughs and pumice made a soft surface for their tent, and lifted it off the ground underneath that was soggy from all the spring snow.

Making improvements to their camp not only made them more physically comfortable, it also kept their minds off fearful thoughts about their scary situation. Even though Paul was there to save them, they still didn't have a solid roof over their head. They still didn't have the luxury of calling for takeout pizza or curling up in a soft warm bed. In survival situations, keeping busy is a great way to free the mind from dwelling on negative thoughts. Working on their camp helped Hannah, Nico and Paul kill time until they could start the trek back to safety.

One of the items Paul had towed in on his sled was a big camp pot. They filled it with snow. It takes a long time to melt snow into drinkable water: A whole big pot full of snow yielded only about an inch of water in the bottom after it melted.

"I can't believe how much snow it takes to make just a tiny bit of water," Nico said.

"Pretty amazing to be able to just turn on the tap water at home, isn't it?" asked Hannah.

"It really is. You don't realize it's so great until you don't have it."

"Well said." Paul smiled. "When you're camping or backpacking, you really start to understand how precious clean water is. We cannot live without it. We could be stuck here for a couple weeks without food, *if we have water*. But a couple days without water and we would die of dehydration, no matter how much food we had. We must have water every day."

"It just flows through the tap like nothing at home. We're *sooo* lucky to have it," said Nico.

"That's for sure. Clean water is a true blessing. It should never be taken for granted. We need to conserve it and be grateful for it. And while supplies are high, you should drink two liters per day."

"You mean like a big soda bottle worth of water? Every day?"

"That's what your body wants. It's one of the best ways

to stay healthy, happy and young! In fact, I even wrote a song about water, would you like to hear it?"

"I sure would! Whoopty doopty doo!" hollered Nico.

The Water Song

The water, so clean and so blue

Love me some water, you're gonna love it too

Flowing in the river, snow accumulates

Condensation soon precipitates

Wherever the water flows, that's where I'll point my nose

Eventually, we're gonna bend for a drink

There can be no life, without water I think

God is in the water, and up in the sky

Swim in the water, sleep high and dry

Wherever the water flows, that's where I'll point my nose and

Wherever the water falls, that's where I'll float my hulls

Swim in the water, drinking the water, love you some water

Water falls white as snow

Ice is water, so are clouds, you know

Life is water, and water is life

But it can smash you to pieces, or cut you like a knife

Wherever the water flows, that's where I'll point my nose and

Wherever the water falls, that's where I'll float my hulls

Swim in the water, drinking the water, love you some water

"Nice," said Nico. "Great song."

"I love that one," said Hannah. She had always been a big fan of Paul's music.

"Thank you so much! There are a lot of things that make this Earth one of the most amazing places in the universe, and water is the main one. Earth is made of over 75% water, and so is the human body. Life as we know it is *not possible* without water. It's more valuable than diamonds!"

Nico looked at him kind of like he was crazy, which wasn't out of the ordinary, because Paul was always saying outlandish things. "Really?" Nico asked with a hint of sarcasm.

"Totally, man. It might not trade at a price like diamonds, but look at this situation. What good would diamonds or gold do you up here, when you are just trying to survive? In these cases, water is so much more valuable than anything! In fact, when scientists look at all the other planets that we can see with telescopes, and when we send robots to Mars, or to orbit other planets, the one thing they want to find is any trace that water *ever* existed there. They've looked everywhere they can and the only place they know of that has this magical liquid is right here on good old planet Earth."

"You mean they can't find water anywhere else?" asked Nico.

"They've found traces of what might be water vapor in some places, and think there might be ice in others. But no pure liquid water anywhere. We've been to the moon. We've put robots on Mars, and we've taken pictures of the planets in our solar system and beyond, and there isn't a river, lake, sea or ocean to be found on any of them. That's why Earth is such a special planet for us. It's made for human survival!"

"Well," Hannah peered into the pot, "is this magical stuff ready for tea, or what?"

* * * * *

Later that night, they relaxed near the campfire under a sky that was packed so full of stars it looked like it was going to burst. To entertain themselves, they had a Fruit Ninja tournament, handing the game back and forth, seeing who could score the highest.

"I know that we need to step away from our devices and screens from time to time. It is interesting that Nico's resistance to the idea is what made it easy for me to find you. Well, not easy, but . . . possible." Paul smiled.

Nico paused his game and looked up. By bringing his phone, he had gone back on his word and hadn't done what he said he was going to do. That made him feel bad, but he couldn't tell if he was being scolded or not.

"It's a good point," Hannah agreed. "You trusted your feelings, Nico, and followed what you love. That's why you have your boots now, and why we have our gear and our friend to help us get out of here."

"Without the GPS, I don't think I would have been able to find you," said Paul.

To Nico, that felt like praise, and it made him smile. It wasn't too often that adults gave him props for going back on his word.

"I get that we can use our devices too much," said Nico. "I don't want to be addicted to them, but I still love them! I just thought, 'Hey, if we have a chance to use it, cool. If not, I'll just enjoy nature.'"

"Technology and nature can go together after all," said Paul. "Our brains and skills are the best survival tools, but it doesn't hurt to be able to call or text. It's better to have a phone and not need it than need a phone and not have it. What's your score, Nico?"

"Hang on," he said, and went back to the game. A few seconds later he finished. "I got 678! I'm the best!"

"It appears you are." Hannah smiled.

CHAPTER 8

They woke up the next day and prepared to go.

Nico put the skins on the bottom of his splitboard. "Dude! Freshies in May!"

"I was thinking," said Paul. "You two didn't make it up to the summit. Maybe we should skin up there and take advantage of this snow."

Backcountry skiing and snowboarding are one of the best ways to find fresh powder. Because of the danger of avalanche, it can be very risky and should only be done with people who have avalanche expertise. Paul was an expert and knew it would be safe. Hannah and Nico didn't have to say anything. The grins that grew across their grills were enough.

* * * * *

Two hours later, they were standing on the summit of the mountain. The sun was shining and it was what Coloradans call a "bluebird" powder day. They were looking down a slope of fresh snow. All around them was nature's finest playground.

Whitecaps of the Rocky Mountains stretched into the distance.

"I never thought we'd be able to ride deep fresh snow in May!" smiled Nico.

"Life is wonderful," said Hannah. "Should we go?"

"Go for it," said Paul. Hannah smiled as Nico nodded for her to go. Hannah, like Nico, was a snowboarder. She dropped in and made big arcing turns, throwing fresh powder up into the air and squealing with delight the whole way. She *ripped* it.

"Thanks for coming to save us, Paul," said Nico.

"The pleasure was all mine, my brother."

"I barely notice how important water is when I'm at home. When I get back, I'm going to really value all the things I have become so used to living with."

"Great idea. Appreciation goes a long way. I appreciate you, my friend. Now get in there and tear up some turns!"

He checked his bindings, clicked the strap on his helmet, smiled and eased over the ridge. At first he pointed it to gain some speed, then he started making tight 's' turns that took him deep into the fresh stash of spring snow.

"Nice!" yelled Paul, and he dropped in. His ski tips dipped in and out of the snow, like a dolphin coming in and out of the water. It was his favorite feeling in the world, and "Whoopty doopty doo!" and hoots and hollers of delight echoed through the valley as the three finished their descent back to civilization.

The End

Download Your Free Copy of *Water* and other RAD songs now!

THE SKY

By Paul Wozniak

Exponential power and endless infinity
Color and character kept by force of gravity

As dynamic as the landscape that it completely encloses
As dull and ugly as a dozen dead roses

The inventor of mathematics and answerer of the riddle
Did God put Earth in the center and humans in the middle?

Does it look the same from Pittsburgh as Bejing?
It is pleasing to notice it is not the same thing

Through its bright reds and blues we always want to fly
I think the best thing about the Earth is the Sky

ALSO AVAILABLE FROM THIS AUTHOR

THE RACE

iPad   iPhone

If I could drive or ride my bike, I'd ride my bike, because that is better.

Nico receives a bike, and with it, some static from the neighborhood bully. So, he stands up for himself and finds himself facing almost impossible odds.

Or Go to www.paulwozniak.com

THE GREEN RADVENTURES™

NICO'S GREEN THUMB

iPad   iPhone

Dig, plant, water, weed, water and the sun provides the heat. When you grow your own food you always have something tasty to eat.

Nico and Hannah plant and enjoy a garden. Join them from spring to fall as they work with the Earth to magically produce their own food. The Green Minstrel (Paul) brings special plants, takes the kids back to Mesopotamia and sings 'Tasty To Eat'.

Or Go to www.paulwozniak.com

THE GREEN RADVENTURES™

NICO GOES TO THE MOUNTAINS

iPad   iPhone

Plastic, cardboard, metal and glass have not yet reached their time to pass. Recycle, complete the cycle, Don't Throw It Out

Reduce, reuse, recycle. Respect! Nico and Hannah take a trip to the landfill and see that it just didn't have to be filled so darn full. The Green Minstrel (Paul) plays 'Don't Throw It Out' and transports them back to a special time in American history.

Or Go to www.paulwozniak.com

ABOUT THE AUTHOR

Paul Wozniak spent a lot of time in the forest as a kid. He still does. There's a little more extreme skiing and a little less "Capture the Flag" these days, but his favorite place to be is still, no contest: outside. A writer since elementary school and an outdoorsman since he could walk, his stories, songs, books, apps and more bring to life his love for the beauty of the backcountry, and illustrate the important idea that we should treat the Earth with the utmost respect.

"Living in Colorado, and Pennsylvania before that, it's so obvious that we have something really special here. I've seen mountains that are bigger than I could imagine and snow slabs that provide water for an entire country. That's why I write these action-adventure books, weaving in these awesome little themes and ideas I've learned from people in the backcountry," Paul says. " This planet is not ordinary. It's beyond extraordinary, and we should protect it, not because we're scared of a disaster, but because we love it and it's the best thing that ever happened to us."

In addition to being an author and recreational athlete, Paul is a popular Colorado DJ, emcee and radio personality. He lives in Fort Collins with his lovely wife Sarah.

Visit www.paulwozniak.com to learn more about Paul's projects that inspire kids (and their grown-ups) to protect our planet.

CPSIA information can be obtained
at www.ICGtesting.com
Printed in the USA
FSOW03n1743091115
13073FS

9 781630 471736